Where Angels Glide at Dawn

Where Angels Glide at Dawn

New Stories from Latin America

Edited by
LORI M. CARLSON
and
CYNTHIA L. VENTURA

Introduction by   Illustrations by
ISABEL ALLENDE   JOSÉ ORTEGA

J. B. LIPPINCOTT   NEW YORK

To my parents, Marie and Robert, who encouraged me to read and dream from the very start, and to my sister, Leigh Ann.

—L.M.C.

•

To the memory of Monserrate, Virgilio, Buenaventura, and Nicolás; my grandparents, who helped me discover the pleasure of a good story; and to M.B.C.

—C.L.V.

Library of Congress Cataloging-in-Publication Data
Where angels glide at dawn : new stories from Latin America / edited by Lori Carlson and Cynthia Ventura ; illustrations by José Ortega.
   p.   cm.
   Summary: A collection of short stories by a variety of Latin American authors.
   ISBN 0-397-32424-3. — ISBN 0-397-32425-1 (lib. bdg.)
   1. Children's stories, Latin American. [1. Short stories. 2. Latin America—Fiction.] I. Carlson, Lori. II. Ventura, Cynthia. III. Ortega, José, date. ill.
PZ5.W523   1990   90-6697
[Fic]—dc20   CIP
                                          AC

Editors' Note

Latin American literature in English translation has been enjoyed by adult readers for over two decades. We think it is time that younger readers also have the opportunity to explore its riches. Since Latin America is a group of countries with a striking variety of climates, geographies, and cultural traditions, we have made every effort to include stories that express this remarkable diversity.

We hope these stories will stimulate the imaginations of our readers and will encourage them to learn more about the cultures, politics, and living conditions that shape the lives of Latin Americans. In order to allow all readers to enjoy the stories, words or phrases that may be unfamiliar are defined in the glossary at the end of the book.

We especially wish to thank Isabel Allende for her introduction, which so poetically evokes five hundred years of Latin American history. We thank Marc Aronson for his valuable editorial suggestions; Ellen Levine and Diana Finch for their enthusiastic support; Miguel Ventura for his generous help; and all the contributors for their kind cooperation.

Lori M. Carlson
Cynthia L. Ventura

CONTENTS

INTRODUCTION

Isabel Allende

A long time ago there was a fabulous land at the end of the world, called America. The European explorers who discovered this land returned to their homes telling everyone that they had seen rivers as wide as oceans, impenetrable jungles, deserts of burning white sand, and mountains so majestic that their peaks reached the highest skies, where angels glided at dawn. They reported that there really were cities of pure gold and human beings who had only one eye on their foreheads and only one foot, so big that during siesta they could raise it over their heads to provide shade.

News of this extraordinary place flew like the wind, awakening people's imagination. To these green coasts came waves of foreigners, some of whom were attracted by adventure, others by interest in science, but the majority by simple greed. They wanted to control everything they could get their hands on, colonize this new continent, and become rich.

First came the *conquistadores*, accompanied by priests whose mission it was to bury forever the native gods: the Plumed Serpent, the Jaguar, the Lord of the Waters, and others. Many peoples of diverse races, who spoke different languages and practiced a variety of customs, lived in this America, but the *conquistadores* had a hard time telling different groups apart and saw them only as people with copper-colored skin, high cheekbones, straight hair, and almond-shaped eyes. Some thought that the natives had no souls and were incapable of feeling pain, so they were treated brutally. For the Indians these were times of great pain and horror. Never before had they suffered so much. Many women refused to have babies so they wouldn't have to grow up as slaves. But for the colonizers these became times of incredible wealth. A poor man who was a beggar in his village in Castile, Spain, could come to America and become a powerful land-owner.

With the passing of time, more soldiers arrived, then traders and merchants, government adminis-trators, pirates and bandits of all kinds, slaves from Africa, immigrants and adventurers from all over the world. These people—Indians, Africans, Europeans, Asians—all mixed together, sweating, crying, lov-ing, all being born under the same sun and dying on the same land. In the end all were *criollos*, of mixed blood and race. The same thing happened with religion, and so gods also coexisted; in the end the Plumed Serpent, Quetzalcoatl, took on the name of a Roman saint, while the Virgin Mary was dressed in Indian beads and African robes. Lan-guages blended together, giving birth to new ac-cents. Spanish lost its hard sounds, Portuguese became musical, English, French, and Dutch became cheerful dialects, and native languages were en-riched with new words. Many of the men and women who were born in the New World forgot their foreign roots and began to dream about a continent that would be free and whose inhabitants would be equal. Despite civil wars, poverty, and vio-lence, for five hundred years that dream has sur-vived in many Latin American hearts.

In the evenings when the stoves were lit for cooking corn, the old family members told stories about the past to their families gathered around. They told fantastic tales because the reality of their land was magical. To tell stories was a daily ritual. Because few people could read and write, storytelling became the only way of preserving their memories. In modern times these tales continued to be passed from one voice to another in those isolated villages not yet reached by radio or television. "Storytellers" haven't disappeared completely in the cities either. Now they are called "writers." Their mission is the same. They speak in their own voices in order to preserve the memory of the past, interpret the events of the present, and imagine the future. In this anthology of stories we can hear their voices brought by a breeze from those magical Latin American lands characterized by their wild geography, violent history, beautiful myths, legends, and people moved by their great passions.

Translated by the editors

THE BEAR'S SPEECH

by
Julio Cortázar

'm the bear in the pipes of the house. I climb through the pipes in the hours of silence, the hot-water pipes, the radiator pipes, the air-conditioning ducts. I go through the pipes from apartment to apartment and I am the bear who goes through the pipes.

I think that they like me because it's my hair that keeps the conduits clean. I run unceasingly through the tubes and nothing pleases me more than slipping through the pipes, running from floor to floor. Once in a while I stick my paw out through a faucet and the girl on the third floor screams that she's scalded herself, or I growl at oven height on the second and Wilhelmina the cook complains that the chimney is drawing badly. At night I go quietly, and it's when I'm moving most quickly that I raise myself to the roof by the chimney to see if the moon is dancing up there, and I let myself slide down like the wind to the boilers in the cellar. And in summer I swim at night in the cistern, prickled all over with the stars; I wash my face first with one paw, then with the other, finally with both together, and that gives me great joy.

Then I slide back down through the pipes of the house, growling happily, and the married couples stir in their beds and deplore the quality of the installation of the pipes. Some even put on the light and write a note to themselves to be sure to remember to complain when they see the superintendent. I look for the tap that's always running in some apartment and I stick my nose out and look into the darkness of rooms where those beings who cannot walk through the pipes live, and I'm always a little sorry for them, heavy beings, big ones, to hear how they snore and dream aloud and are so very much alone. When they wash their faces in the morning, I caress their cheeks and lick their noses and I leave, somewhat sure of having done some good.

Buenos Aires, Argentina's capital city, is one of the largest cities in Latin America. The author was from Argentina and this story could be set in Buenos Aires.

Translated by Paul Blackburn

The original title of the English translation of this story is "The Discourse of the Bear"

THE REBELLION OF THE MAGICAL RABBITS

by
Ariel Dorfman

When the wolves conquered the land of the rabbits, the first thing the leader of the pack did was to proclaim himself King. The second was to announce that the rabbits had ceased to exist. Now and forever it would be forbidden to even mention their name.

Just to be on the safe side, the new Wolf King went over every book in his realm with a big black pencil, crossing out words and tearing out pictures of cottontails until he was satisfied that not a trace of his enemies remained.

But an old gray fox who was his counselor brought bad news.

"The birds, Your Wolfiness, insist that they have seen some . . . some of those creatures. From on high."

"So how come I don't see anything from way up here, on my throne?" asked the Wolf.

"In times like these," answered the fox, "people have got to see to believe."

"Seeing is believing? Bring me that monkey who takes photos, the one who lives nearby. I'll teach those birds a lesson."

The monkey was old and weak.

"What can the Wolf of all Wolves want with me?" he asked, looking at his wife and daughter.

The little girl had an answer. "He must want you to take a picture of the rabbits, Dad."

"Quiet, quiet," said her mother. "Rabbits don't exist."

But the little monkey knew that rabbits did exist. It was true that, since the howling wolves had invaded the country, the rabbits no longer came to visit her as they had before. But in her dreams she continued hearing the green rain of their voices singing nearby, reflecting in her head as if she were a pond under the moonlight, and when she awoke there was always a small gift beside her bed. Walls and closed doors were like water for the rabbits.

"That's why I sleep well," said the little girl. "That's why that General Wolf must need the photo. To keep nightmares away. You'll bring me a picture of them someday, won't you, Dad?"

The monkey felt fear crawl up and down his fur. "Send this little girl to her room," he told his wife, "until she understands that there are certain things we just don't talk about."

The King of the Wolves was not in the best of moods when the monkey came in. "You're late. And I'm in a hurry. I need photographs of each important act in my life. And all my acts, let me tell you, are supremely important. . . . Can you guess what we're going to do with those pictures? You can't? We're going to put one on every street, inside every bush, in every home. I'll be there, watching each citizen with my very own eyes. You'd better pity those who don't have the latest events of my life hung up on their walls. And you know who is going to distribute each picture? You don't know?"

The monkey was trembling so hard that no words came out.

"The birds, ugly monkey. Now they'll bite their own beaks before they twitter around with any nonsense about rabbits. And we'll tie an endless cord to their legs, so they can't escape. Understand?"

The monkey understood so well that his trembling paw immediately clicked the shutter of the camera, taking the first picture.

"Go," roared the Wolf, "and develop it. I want it on every wall in the kingdom."

But when the photographer returned some minutes later, he did not dare to enter the throne room, and asked one of the soldiers to call the counselor. Without a word, the monkey passed him the picture he had just taken.

The fox blinked once, and then blinked again. In a corner of the photo, far from the muscular, ferocious figure of the King—who had both arms up in the air as if he had just won a boxing championship—appeared what was without any doubt the beginning of an ear, the ear of someone who had insolently come to spy on the whole ceremony.

"You blind monkey!" fumed the fox. "How come you didn't notice that this . . . this thing was there? Can't you focus that camera of yours?"

"If it could get into the picture," the monkey answered, "it was because you and your guards let it get close."

"It won't happen again," the counselor promised. "Rub out that . . . ear before His Wolfishness finds out."

From his bag, the monkey took out a special liquid that he used to erase any detail that might bother a client. The intruding ear began to disappear as if it had never existed.

The King of the Wolves was pleased with the portrait and ordered it sent all over the realm. Two hours later he personally went on an inspection tour to make sure that not a window was without a picture of his large, gleaming, dangerous grin. "Not bad," he said, "but this photo is already getting old. People should see my latest deeds. Take another. Quick. Show me scaring these pigeons—right away. And bring it to me immediately. You took too long last time."

But the monkey wasn't able to comply this time either. Once again he had the counselor called secretly.

"Again?" asked the fox. "It happened again?"

Except that now it was worse than an indiscreet ear. A whole corner of the new picture was filled with the unmistakable face of . . . yes, there was no denying it, of a rabbit winking an eye in open defiance of the nearby guards.

"We've got to tighten security," muttered the fox. "Meanwhile, erase that invader."

"Wonderful," shouted the King Wolf when finally

he was given the picture. "Look at the frightened faces of the pigeons trying to escape. I want a million copies. I want them on milk cartons and on the coupons inside cereals. . . . Onward. Onward. Let's go and smash up a dam. Come on, monkey. Fame awaits us both."

The beavers had been working summer and winter for three years on a beautiful dam that would allow them to irrigate a distant valley.

The Wolf of Wolves climbed a tree. "I want you to shoot the precise moment when my feet crash into the middle of the dam, monkey. If you miss the shot, next time I'll fall on top of you and then I'll have to get myself another photographer. Are you ready?"

Not only was the monkey ready, so was the counselor. The fox was breathing down the old monkey's back, peering over his shoulder, watching, listening. Nothing could escape those vigilant, darting eyes. Not a fuzzy ear would dare to make its appearance.

So neither the monkey nor the fox could believe it when, a bit later, they saw at the bottom of the picture a rabbit lolling on his side as if he were relaxing at a picnic. Next to him, another rabbit had raised her paw and was boldly thumbing her nose.

"This is an epidemic," said the fox. "And let me tell you, our lives are in danger."

"Let's start erasing," the monkey said wearily.

"You erase. I'll get a squadron of buzzards and hawks. They see all animals, even the quick and the small."

His Wolfhood the King yelped with pleasure when he saw the picture. It portrayed him at the exact moment he was breaking the backbone of the beavers' dam. In the distance, families of beavers could be seen fleeing. There was not a single shadow of a rabbit.

"Send it out! A strong country is an educated country, a country that always is tuned in to the latest news. What are we going to do now for some fun?"

"We could rest," the monkey suggested, his paws peeling from the harsh erasing fluid.

The Wolf looked at him as if he were a stone.

"And who asked you for an opinion? I'm in charge here. That's why I was born with these teeth, and you'd better pray you never have to feel them crunching your bones. Onward. We are the future, the morrow, the dawn! We'll go on until there's no more light."

But in each new photo, the rabbits became more

plentiful, audacious, and saucy. His Wolfinity the King destroyed sugar mills, shook squirrels out of their trees and hid their nuts, stripped ducks of their feathers, drove sheep off cliffs, drilled holes in the road so that horses would break their legs, unveiled new cages and old dungeons . . . and the more his frightening yellow eyes flickered, the more innumerable were the rabbits of every color that frolicked in the margins of the photographs. Even the clouds seemed full of fur and whiskers and cottontails.

"Hey, birdie," jeered the Supreme Wolf, grabbing a swallow about to fly off with a bag overflowing with pictures, "what tune are you singing now, featherhead? Who's that in the center of the picture, huh? Who's the King?"

The bird held his beak tight, so that not even a peep could come out.

"Lights, camera, action, monkey!" the Monarch demanded. "Call this: WOLF KING RECEIVES HOMAGE FROM A MESSENGER."

The monkey obeyed, but could hardly hide his despair. Though nobody ever saw the rebels when the photos were taken, they were always there when it was time to show them, nibbling lettuce at the very feet of the biggest and baddest of wolves.

"Exterminate them," hissed the fox, who had ordered a stronger, more acid liquid. "Don't leave even a twitch of a nose."

But the pictures were beginning to look defective. There were blank spaces everywhere. The monkey knew that the only solution was to convince His Wolfiness to sit up high on an elevated throne. Since rabbits live underground, they wouldn't be able to wiggle their way into the frame of the photograph.

The King, fortunately, was delighted with the idea. "I'll look more impressive up here. And I can keep an eye on those birds. What a surprise for my subjects when they find my new picture at breakfast, right? So get here early, monkey, do you hear?"

When the exhausted monkey dragged himself home, his fingers hurting from the terrible liquid, the latest photograph of the King had just been plastered on the front door of his house. Just at that moment, a soldier was leaving.

"No cause for alarm, Mr. Monkey," the soldier laughed. "Just a routine inspection to see if anybody is sabotaging His Wolfhood's pictures."

The monkey rushed inside. "Our daughter? Is she all right? Did she say anything?"

"I'm fine, Dad," the little girl said. "Those wolves are gone, aren't they? And you brought me that special photo—you know, the one I asked you for?"

The monkey felt as if from all four walls, from all four pictures on the four walls, the eight eyes of the Biggest of Wolves were watching each word he might say.

"Let your father rest," said her mother. "The only pictures he's taken are the ones we've put up in the house, like good citizens."

But the next morning, the monkey was awakened by his child's kiss. She put her lips near his ears and whispered something so softly that only he could hear it: "Thank you. It's the best present you could ever give me. You're a magical dad."

"Thanks? Thanks for what?"

She motioned almost imperceptibly toward the wall from which the photo of the Wolf King ruled. Her father opened his eyes wide. In one of the corners of that picture, like the sun rising over the mountains, he could just glimpse, in the act of making their gradual but glorious appearance, a pair of, yes, of course, a pair of soft, pink, pointed ears.

The monkey jumped out of bed. The liquid he had applied did not work permanently. The rabbits had needed the whole night to sneak back into the pictures, but somehow they had managed it.

"I think they knew I was scared," the little girl murmured, " and came to see me while I slept."

Her father dressed in less time than it takes a chill to run up a spine and scurried to the palace without stopping for breakfast. Was this happening only at their house or could the same invasion have taken place everywhere in the kingdom? If so, how could the rabbits be removed from so many portraits?

His Wolfiness was still in bed, but the counselor was already pacing about, biting the tip of his tail. "It's a plague," he said, "but, fortunately, it is already under control. The offending pictures have been burned. As for you . . ."

"I swear that I—"

"Not a word from you," interrupted the fox. "It's lucky those creatures don't exist. Imagine the damage they'd cause if they really existed. But enough talk. What we need now is a new photo to replace the ones that are contaminated."

They rushed to the new throne, which was now set up on top of four colossal wooden legs, out of reach of the spreading virus of the mischievous ears.

"I want two shots," His Wolfhood demanded, "one of me ascending my throne and another of me sitting on it, enjoying the fresh air. And send them abroad too, so those silly foreign papers will stop attacking me."

This time, when the photos were developed, there

was no trouble. Not so much as a carrot of a sign of a rabbit.

"Didn't I tell you? Didn't I tell you they don't exist?" The counselor was jubilant. "It was just a matter of your focusing the camera properly."

For the next few days, there were no more unpleasant surprises. The Wolf of Wolves felt happy, high above the heads of the multitude. He let his lieutenants run things while he posed for pictures giving commands, delivering speeches, signing laws. He examined the shots carefully, however. "Congratulations," he said. "You're being more careful, monkey. It seems you're learning your trade just by being near me. I don't see any more of those whitish spots that spoiled my first pictures."

But one morning, the monkey was again awakened by his daughter's voice. "They're back, Dad," she whispered in his ears. "Those pictures you took sure are magical."

In one set of photos, at the foot of the towering throne, a small army of rabbits was biting, chewing, and splintering the wooden legs. Their teeth worked patiently, and they stopped their work only now and again to wave to the spectators.

The counselor was waiting. The monkey could see his fur ruffling and swelling like a swarm of bees.

"How many this time?" the monkey asked.

"The photos are being taken care of," the fox said grimly. "But the birds have got wind of what happened, and now they're telling everyone that those . . . those awful animals exist. And His Wolfinity is beginning to suspect something. 'Why are those birds so happy, so shrill?' he asks. I told him they're just a bunch of featherbrains, full of hot air."

"What did he answer?" asked the monkey.

The King had announced that balloons are full of hot air too and that they could be popped. If those birds didn't keep quiet, he would make them disappear.

But the counselor had another idea: The Wolf of All Wolves should tie a recording of one of his latest speeches around the necks of the birds. They would have to carry not only the photos, but also the King's words, all over his kingdom. Nobody would be able to hear any of their songs.

"Hearing is believing," trumpeted His Wolfiness. "We'll give them a taste of some hymns, some military marches, some lessons in history, economics, and ethics."

The old monkey's life became unbearable. Not even the recorded howls of the King and his chorus of warlike beasts could stop the timid appearance, in the next photo, of an inquisitive nose, a pair of furry ears, some white whiskers, and something hungry gnawing away at the legs of the throne.

The fox replaced the chief officer of the royal guard with a boa constrictor straight from the jungle of a neighboring country. He put small, hundred-eyed spiders in strategic places throughout the Wolfdom. One day he ordered half the population to shave off their shiny fur so that no spy could hide in it. To punish the cows, accused of uttering subversive moos, he commanded that their milk be soured. And finally, he raised the volume of the King's broadcasts. But in spite of these efforts, there began to be heard a persistent, rowdy, merry sound, the clicking of thousands of tiny teeth, the burbling of an underground stream.

The monkey felt dizzy.

The rhythm was maddening. During the night, the legs of the throne, spindlier by the minute, were reinforced grudgingly by woodpeckers who would have much preferred to take the throne apart. The monkey had to rely on every photographic trick of the trade, now erasing, now trimming with scissors, disguising ears so they looked like shadows and shadows so they looked like wallpaper. He even began using old portraits of the King, trying to make them seem like recent ones.

Until one night, when it was very late, the old monkey was awakened by an angry hand that shook him from his slumber. It was the counselor, flanked by a fierce escort of soldiers. The Lord Wolf had sent for him.

The whole house was up by now. The little girl watched her father begin dressing.

"Say hello to His Foxcellency," said the monkey.

"Dad," she said, and it was astonishing that she did not speak in a low, fearful voice anymore, as if the armed guards were not even there, "today you've got to bring me that picture I asked for."

"A picture?" The counselor showed interest. "A picture of what, of whom?"

The child continued to ignore him. "Today you'll bring me a photo of the rabbits, right, Dad? For my wall?"

The mother monkey touched the girl's head as if she had fever. "Hasn't your father told you that rabbits don't exist? Haven't we shut you up in your room for telling lies?"

"They exist," the girl announced. "Everybody knows they exist."

"Just as I suspected," said the counselor. "Let's go."

The Wolfiest of Wolves was waiting for them atop his throne. Around each leg, hundreds of guards and snakes kept watch.

"Monkey, you are a traitor," thundered the King. "Your photos are being used by people who say that strange and malicious creatures—who are non-existent as everyone knows—are conspiring this very night to overthrow my rule. They say my throne trembles and my dynasty will topple. Is there any evidence that my throne trembles? Does anybody dare say so?" And he yowled like a hundred jet fighters in the air. "We'll start by making a recording of that sound. And you, you monkey, you're going to help me stamp out these rumors. Touching is believing. You are going to make me a wide-angle, three-dimensional picture that will cover all walls. In color. Because I am going to crown myself Emperor of the Wolves, the Supreme Wolferor. And if a single wretched rabbit shows its snout, I will make you eat the photos, one by one, a million of them, and then I'll eat you and not only you, but your wife and your daughter, and all the monkeys in this country. Now. Take that picture."

The monkey stuck his quaking head under the

black cloth behind his camera and focused on the throne. He let out a little moan. Up till then, the rabbits had appeared only later, when the picture was developed. But here they were now, directly in front of his lens, ungovernable and carefree, gnawing away, biting not only the wood of the throne, but also the swords of the astonished guards and the very rattles of the rattlesnakes.

"What's the matter?" bellowed the future Wolferor, who was not looking downward so his profile would be perfect for posterity.

The monkey moved the camera nearer the throne, hoping the rabbit army would not come out in the picture. The rabbits moved faster than he did. They were clambering up the legs, one on top of the other as if they were monkeys or birds. The soldiers tried to frighten them away in silence, unwilling to attract the attention of the King, but the invaders were too agile. The Wolves kept bumping into one another and hitting each other over the head. The monkey realized that a contingent of birds had arrived from above, winging freely through the air, without a cord tied to them or a recording.

"Hurry up!" ordered the Wolf of all Wolves.

The monkey closed his eyes very tightly. It was better not to witness what was going to happen.

At the very moment he clicked the shutter, he heard a deafening noise. He knew what he was going to see when he opened his eyes, but still could not believe it: Like an old elm tree rotten to the core, the throne had come crashing to the ground along with the King of Wolves, guards, snakes, counselor, and all. The monkey blinked. There at the foot of his tripod lay the Biggest, Baddest, the Most Boastful Wolf in the Universe. His ribs were broken, his black fur was torn by the fall, his yellow eyes were reddened, and he was wailing in pain.

"Monkey," squeaked the would-be Wolferor of the World, "this picture . . . you have my permission not to publish it."

At that moment, all the lights in the palace went out. The monkey was paralyzed. He did not know where to go. Then, as if someone in the darkness were suddenly shining a light on a pathway, he knew what he must do. He grabbed his camera and his bag, and clutching them to his chest like a treasure, he fled.

His daughter was waiting for him at the door of the house.

"Wait," he said to her. "Wait. I've brought you something." And without another word, he raced into his darkroom to develop the last picture as quickly as possible.

When he came out a few minutes later, his daughter and wife were standing on chairs, taking down the pictures of the Wolf King.

"Here," the old monkey said to his daughter, blinking in the bright light. "Here, this is the picture you've been asking for all this time. I've finally brought you your present."

"Thanks, Dad," the little girl said. "But I don't need it anymore."

She pointed around the room and toward the street and across the fields where the sun was beginning to rise.

The world was full of rabbits.

Chile, the long, thin country on the Pacific coast of South America, is the setting of this story, which describes a time when a dictatorship did not allow some people to describe the events they saw happening around them.

This story is the author's English adaptation of the original story in Spanish entitled "La Rebelión de los Conejos Mágicos."

THE DAY WE WENT TO SEE SNOW

by
Alfredo Villanueva-Collado

From the first moment I heard on the radio that the Lady Mayor was going to give the children of San Juan the best Christmas present they had ever received, I knew that my greatest and deepest wish would be granted: I was going to see that beautiful, white stuff that covered houses on the Christmas cards our relatives sent us from their neighborhood in New York called "El Barrio." The radio finally announced the date, time, and place, and that whole week I had to put up with my mom and dad, who teased me because it had occurred to me to ask for a pair of skis for the great event.

The day had come. I woke up suddenly with the sun bursting through the louvered windows. I could hear Mom in the kitchen fixing breakfast, Dad taking a shower in the bathroom, Roberto searching through the drawers in his room. I remembered what day it was and my heart started to beat faster. I ran to the bathroom to wash up and get dressed. I decided to wear a cream-colored sweater, corduroy pants, and thick socks. Mom started laughing when she saw me dressed like that. Dad looked tired and grumbled that it was too hot and that maybe it wasn't worth making the trip. "There's going to be a terrible traffic jam," he said, not really talking to anybody in particular.

Mom added, "It's already nine o'clock and it's going to take us two hours to get to San Juan. People make a big fuss out of nothing. We better hurry."

Roberto and I sat in the backseat of the car. We each had a window. Mom reminded us of what would happen if we didn't sit still. And as she scolded us, she pointed with her long, immaculately manicured, dark-red nails. It was her way of keeping us under control.

Leaving Bayamón was easy, but when we reached

28

Santurce the traffic jam was unbelievable. We moved four feet every half hour. The heat and humidity made the inside of the car feel as sticky as a steam bath. Roberto pretended to be shooting Indians; that day he wore his cowboy outfit with a wide-brimmed hat and a holster. *"Bang!"* and an Indian fell. *"Bang!"* Another one fell. Mom noticed the horrified faces of the people in the other cars stewing in their steam baths. She turned around suddenly, grabbed Roberto by the arm, and told him to stop playing around, that it was rude to point at people, especially with a gun.

Then she let Roberto go and looked at me to see what I was doing. But my game didn't bother anybody. I loved counting the various makes of cars, especially Studebakers, which really wasn't that easy in that traffic jam. But I could do it without attracting too much attention. A Ford went by and up ahead was a Chrysler. There were lots of Chevrolets and every once in a while a Cadillac, but I couldn't find a Studebaker for anything in the world. I inched up slowly to look through the rear windshield when suddenly, *bam!* A hand pushed me down into my seat. I was warned that if we all died in an accident it would be because Dad had not been able to see through the rear windshield with me in the way. *I* and only *I* would be responsible.

We finally reached the bridges in Condado. A slight breeze helped the itch that was spreading all over my body. I was sweaty and wanted to take off my sweater, but Mom, who had eyes in the back of her head, told me that I would get a chill and end up in the hospital with pneumonia. Besides, I would get a spanking because decent people don't take their clothing off in public. Roberto's situation was even worse: He had an itch in a funny place, which he tried to scratch without anybody noticing. When he couldn't stand it anymore, he jerked forward, leaving a sweaty spot on the red plastic seat next to the window. He was warned that he would go cross-eyed if he continued scratching that part of his body. The radio was on, announcing the magnificence of the gift made by the great Mayor of San Juan to her people. This only made Dad angrier. "Too many people. Who would ever think of bringing that stuff here so that all these idiots can think that they are Eskimos for a day?"

But Mom lectured him: "Look, you were the one who promised the kids. If it weren't for you, we wouldn't be in this traffic jam! I think we should leave the car here and walk to the park. But you're too lazy and you don't want to walk even though we're so close."

As if by magic, we saw a parking spot, and Dad, who was furious by now, parked the car with one swift turn of the steering wheel. "Are you sure this is a legal spot?" asked Mom, always afraid of breaking the law.

"What a nightmare," answered Dad, who didn't feel like talking anymore. We got out. Mom and Dad walked in front, he wearing a *guayabera* shirt and she had a shawl draped over her shoulders, "just in case." Roberto and I walked together; he skipped along and tugged at his cowboy pants, which had become torture, while I battled with my sweater, which scratched like sandpaper. It was almost noon, when the sun was hottest.

In the park we made our way through the surging crowd. Millions of kids, dressed in Levi's, corduroys, gloves, and even strange red ski caps, were shrieking. In the center of this excitement was the white, or almost white, bright, melting snow. I ran toward it, smearing my pants with mud from the melted snow and the dirt tracked in by the shoes of the people who had come from all over the island. I touched the snow. It wasn't so great after all. In fact, it occurred to me that I could make some in the freezer at home if I really wanted to. What a mess, and for what? But obviously everyone else thought it was wonderful. People went crazy. They walked around the pile of snow with their eyes popping out, while the kids splashed in the mud or posed for their parents' Kodak cameras. To one side, on a platform, stood the mayor who had made this miracle possible. Her famous white hair was done up in a bun that looked like a snowman. She was smiling and fanning herself with one of her many lace fans.

What should have been a refreshing day did nothing to improve Dad's mood, because when I looked at him he was almost purple with rage. He was holding a screaming Roberto, whose pants and holster had settled around his knees. I rushed over to them and slipped on the slush, falling only five inches away from Mom's fingernails. She pulled me up, inspected what was left of my sweater, and said "Wait until we get home."

To make matters worse, when we finally remembered where Dad had left the car, there was a parking ticket on the windshield.

This story takes place in the Caribbean island of Puerto Rico. Since 1898, Puerto Rico has been a commonwealth, also called a "Free

Associated State," of the United States. In 1952, the mayor of the capital city, San Juan, Felisa Rincón de Gautier, brought snow in an airplane from the United States mainland to the children of Puerto Rico.

Translated by Cynthia L. Ventura

Adapted from "El Día Que Fuimos a Mirar la Nieve"

WITH MY EYES CLOSED

by
Reinaldo Arenas

I'm going to tell you what happened to me yesterday because I know that you're not going to laugh or yell at me. But not my mom. I won't tell my mom anything, because if I do, she will scold me and give me a hard time. And even though she's probably right, I don't want want to hear any advice or warnings. That's why I'm going to tell you everything, because I know you're not going to say anything.

Since I'm eight years old, I have to go to school every day. The alarm clock my Aunt Angela gave me wakes me up early every morning because my school is pretty far away.

At around six in the morning Mom starts nagging at me to get up and at seven I'm sitting on my bed rubbing my eyes. Then I have to do everything in a hurry: put my clothing on, run to school, and make a mad dash to get into line because they've already rung the school bell and the teacher is standing at the door.

But yesterday was different because Aunt Angela had to go to Oriente and she was going to take a train before 7:00 A.M. There was a lot of confusion in the house. All the neighbors came to say good-bye to her, and Mom was so nervous that when she was about to pour boiling water through a coffee filter, she dropped the kettle on the floor and burned her foot.

I had no choice but to wake up with that intolerable racket. Since I was now awake, I decided to get up and this is when all my troubles started.

Aunt Angela, after many kisses and hugs, finally left. I took off immediately for school even though it was still pretty early.

"Today I don't have to run," I thought happily. And I started walking slowly. When I was about to cross the street, I tripped over a cat that was lying on the curb. "What a place to sleep," I said, and I touched it with the tip of my shoe. But it didn't move. Then I squatted next to it and confirmed that it was dead. "Poor thing," I thought. It had probably been run over by a car and had been put on the curb by someone so the cars wouldn't keep running over it. What a shame, because it was a big and yellow cat that was probably too young to die. Well, what can you do? So I continued walking.

Since it was still early, I went to the candy store, because even though it was far away from school, they always had fresh and delicious candies. In front of this candy store there were two old ladies, each one with a small basket and her hand extended, begging. Once, I gave each one a nickel and the two of them said "Bless you" to me in unison. That made me laugh and I put another two nickels in those wrinkled and freckled hands. And the two of them repeated "Bless you" but this time it wasn't as funny. And ever since, every time I go by there, they look at me with expectation and I have no choice but to give each one a nickel. I really couldn't give them anything yesterday, since I had spent my last quarter on chocolate cupcakes. And this is why I went out the back door, so the old ladies wouldn't see me.

I only had to cross the bridge and walk two blocks to get to school.

I stood on that bridge for a moment because I

heard a lot of noise below, at the river's edge. I held on to the handrail and looked down. A group of kids of all ages had trapped a river rat and were yelling and throwing rocks at it. The rat ran from one side to the other, but there was no escape and it squealed loudly and desperately. Then one of the kids picked up a large piece of bamboo and hit the rat hard, on its back, squashing it. The rest of the kids ran to where the rodent was. They were yelling and jumping triumphantly as they threw it into the river. But the dead rat didn't sink. It continued floating on its back until it was dragged away by the current.

The kids took their noise to another part of the river. And I continued walking.

"It's so easy to walk on the bridge," I thought. I can do it with my eyes closed, since on one side there are bars that prevent you from falling into the water, and on the other side the curb warns you when you're going to step into the street. And to prove it, I closed my eyes and continued walking. At the beginning I was holding on to the handrail with one hand, but after a little while, I didn't need it anymore. I continued walking with my eyes closed, but don't tell my mom. With your eyes closed, you can see many things and even see better than when your eyes are open. . . . The first thing I saw was a big yellow cloud that was brighter than other clouds; it looked like the sun when it's setting behind trees. Then I closed my eyes even tighter and a reddish cloud turned blue. But not only blue, green and purple too. A bright purple like the purple in the rainbow when it's rained a lot and the land is almost soaked.

And, with my eyes closed, I started thinking about all kinds of things. I didn't stop walking. I saw my Aunt Angela leaving the house, not in the red dotted dress she always wore when she went to Oriente, but in a long, white dress. And she was so tall, she looked like a telephone pole wrapped in a sheet. But she looked nice.

I continued walking and I tripped over a cat on the curb. But this time, when I touched it with the tip of my shoe, it jumped and ran away. The bright yellow cat ran away because it was alive and it got scared when I woke it up. And I laughed a lot when I saw it disappear, with its arched back looking as if it were shooting sparks.

I continued walking, with my eyes closed, of course. And this was how I arrived at the candy store. But since I couldn't buy any candy because I had spent my last quarter, I was happy just looking at the candy through the shop window. And this is what I was doing, admiring the candies, when I heard two voices behind the counter ask me: "Do you want a candy?" And when I looked up, I realized that the two salesladies were the two old ladies who were always begging at the candy store's entrance. I didn't know what to say. But they seemed to guess what I wanted. They smiled, and took out a big chocolate-almond cake and put it in my hands.

I was very happy with that enormous cake and walked out of the store.

When I was walking on the bridge with the cake in my hands, I again heard the noise the kids were making. And (with my eyes closed) I looked over the handrail on the bridge and saw them swimming quickly toward the middle of the river to save a water rat because it appeared that the poor thing was sick and couldn't swim.

The kids took the trembling rat out of the water and put it on a rock so it could dry off in the sun. Then I called them so we could all eat the chocolate-almond cake. I couldn't eat that big cake alone.

I really was about to call them, and I even lifted the cake up high so they could see it and wouldn't think I was lying. They came running, but at that moment, *crash!* A truck hit me in the middle of the street, which is where I had been standing without knowing it.

And here I am, with my legs in white casts. They are as white as the walls in this room where ladies walk in wearing white uniforms to give me a shot or a pill that also happens to be white.

And don't think that what I've told you is a lie. Don't think that because I have a little fever and every once in a while I complain about pain in my legs that I'm lying. And if you want to see if it's true or not, go to the bridge. It's probably still there, all squashed on the asphalt, that enormous chocolate-almond cake given to me by the two smiling old ladies.

Cuba is the largest island in the Caribbean Sea and is only ninety miles south of Florida. Life in Cuba changed dramatically in 1959 when a communist government came to power. Many older Cubans, whether they still live on the island or in other countries, date their lives to before and after this event.

Translated by Cynthia L. Ventura

THE CAVE

by
Enrique Jaramillo Levi

A white dog with dark spots was sniffing around a fire hydrant in front of the store window. On the other side of the window, the shapes of objects looked blurred. I opened the door to my father's store and a little bell rang. When I was about to enter, I had the distinct impression that a large, cavernous mouth was going to swallow me. I went inside anyway.

I was welcomed by my cat. My sweet cat. His sad, crossed eyes looked at me tamely as he arched his back. Yellow, blue, and white neon lights flickered on and off. The walls had the familiar scents of incense and pine. I hesitated for a moment. I looked behind the counter and saw that my father was busy helping a client who looked Chinese. I continued walking toward that place I had been told many times not to enter.

After walking down the long hallway lined with old chests and forgotten furniture, I entered "the cave." That was what my older brother called it. He would tell me, "Dad stores all kinds of strange things in there. Every time I go inside, it seems that the stuffed crocodiles look at me as if they're unhappy. I wonder why those crocodiles are in the cellar. They're probably just iguanas or gigantic lizards Dad's collected."

All kinds of old clothing that looked like theater costumes hung on hooks randomly nailed into the walls of the cellar. I touched the silk, worn and dirty, and a horrible spider almost bit me. I screamed once and just then the little white wooden horse with the broken leg, which had disappeared mysteriously a long time ago, rocked forward, greeting me happily from his corner covered with cobwebs. The mild breeze that filtered through the airshaft gently swayed a piece of salted codfish that hung from the ceiling on a wire. I don't know what made me stretch out my hand at that moment and pull off a piece of that dark, leathery skin and chew on it, tasting the salt that reminded me of seas sailed by pirates.

I continued walking into the darkness. I sensed shadows moving in the back of the room and heard small, squeaky sounds. I started fighting the fear I was feeling and my heart started pounding like crazy. I felt strange sensations on my skin and I didn't know if it was just my imagination or if they were caused by spirits I couldn't see. I stopped to listen. Yes, now it was loud. I heard a screech. I lifted my foot; it became completely silent in the cave.

Twisted wires hanging out of boxes created strange shapes. Foul smells seeped from ancient bottles and made me feel dizzy. I suddenly saw the beady eyes of a huge rat. I screamed and saw them fade in the darkness. I felt strange things bumping into my ankles, and I took a step back. And another. I tripped on some rolled-up wire that I thought was a rattlesnake coiling around my feet. I wanted to run, but I tripped and fell into a box that was inside another larger box. I felt very small. And in fact I was, because I saw the enormous eyes of my cat shining like streetlights in the darkness. They stared at me for a long time, hypnotically, as if everything had suddenly stopped forever. The cat stretched out his big front paws and placed them on the edge of the larger box, breaking that strange trance we were in. As he was stretching, he lowered that gigantic, threatening head. I saw myself reflected in those liquid pools that continued staring at me. "It's me . . . Anita!" I said, trying to calm him down. But he opened his mouth wide. I was disgusted by the smell of codfish on his breath.

I saw the sharp points of his fangs coming closer. I could see them slowly penetrating the darkness. In one swift movement, I managed to grab onto one of the long, elastic hairs of his whiskers and swing on it with the hope of being able to jump out of the box. I closed my eyes so I wouldn't tremble before those bewildered crossed eyes that were right in front of me, that continued watching me sway from side to side.

I let go of his whisker and fell on the rolled-up wire, which wrapped itself around me. I couldn't move. I was a tiny doll trapped in a whirlpool of metallic waves that vibrated like shiny, new springs. A loud meow made me look up. His wide, dark mouth with sharp fangs was getting closer.

Suddenly a light was turned on. The cat ran away. My father's strong hands started to unravel the wires that had me trapped. I looked up at his face for some kind of an explanation, a signal. I saw only his usual expression, as if nothing out of the ordinary had happened. He helped me stand up and I brushed off the dust trying to get rid of the bad memories. Everything went back to normal. I confirmed this when the mirror on the wall reflected my normal height. But my bones ached. They felt strange, taut, and hot inside. A little bell rang. I knew a new customer was coming in. Dad left and made a gesture with his hand for me to follow him. Before leaving, I wanted to look at myself in the mirror one more time. I saw the cat approach me from behind. As usual, I was at least three times as big as he. Then the cat meowed. I turned around to face him. His crossed eyes shone under the light that hung from the ceiling. "You're not a bad kitten . . . are you?" I whispered. I felt the heat tingling in my bones. As my cat walked away, swaying his impertinent tail, I'm sure I saw him wink at me.

For weeks after, I felt a lot of pain in my bones when it rained, especially at night. I never again went near cats. My brother thinks that I fell asleep in the cave that day and had a bad nightmare. Of course that is the most logical explanation. Anybody would say that.

But only I know that even today, so many years later, when it rains a lot and it's cold, I still get under the covers, afraid to look at myself in the mirror.

This story takes place in Panama, a Central American country on the Isthmus of Panama, which borders both the Atlantic and Pacific oceans. Ships from around the world pass through its canal.

Translated by Cynthia L. Ventura

PALETÓN
AND THE
MUSICAL ELEPHANT

by
Jorge Ibargüengoitia

M r. Paletón was a fat millionaire who was used to getting everything he wanted. Every morning, before getting up from bed, he would scratch his belly, look up at the ceiling, and ask himself: "Paletón, what do you feel like buying today?"

In this way he put together the most complete collection of automobiles in the world, the most famous pianos, and an unequaled collection of doorknobs. He also had several notable animals, like Eloísa, the flea that wore clothing; Porrón, the mathematician bear; and Policarpo, an animal that didn't look like any other animal because it had five

51

legs, two heads, and nothing that even resembled a snout. He kept all of these things in his house, which had so many rooms, no one could ever count them.

One morning, after scratching his belly and asking himself the usual question, Paletón thought: "I want to buy Paco, the musical elephant at Chapultepec Park."

Paco is one of the largest elephants in the world. He's ten and a half feet tall and weighs six tons. He has tusks that are a yard long and every day he eats eleven pounds of papaya decorated with walnuts and hazelnuts. But the most striking thing about Paco is his trunk; it is so sensitive and agile that he can use it to play the piano and give concerts. His favorite pieces are Pavlova's *Gavotte* and Ravel's *Concert for the Left Hand*.

Paletón got out of bed, put on his emerald-green silk robe, and made a phone call to Chapultepec Park to say that he wanted to buy the musical elephant and to ask how much he cost. They answered that they wouldn't sell the elephant for any price.

Paletón had a fit and rolled on the floor. When he was finally calm, he understood that all wasn't lost and that there was a way to get what he wanted. He hung up the phone again and dialed a number.

"Hello? Are you the Chicago gangsters? How much will you charge me for kidnapping the musical elephant at Chapultepec Park and bringing him to my house?"

"Five million pesos," answered the gangsters.

"You got a deal," said Paletón, and hung up.

The Chicago gangsters were five big-headed, short guys who lived in the same house. When someone hired them for a job, they put on hats and scarves and sat around a table eating spaghetti and planning the robbery.

Between mouthfuls, each one suggested how it should be done. The most hardworking one suggested building a tunnel that would connect the house where they lived to the zoo. The silliest one, who thought that elephants were made of rubber, suggested they let the air out of Paco and take him out of the zoo in a suitcase. Finally, the smartest one had his turn: "I think there's a simpler way to do it. Tonight, Paco is giving a concert at Bellas Artes Concert Hall. How do you take an elephant from Chapultepec Park to Bellas Artes? Very simple. In a moving van. I propose we arrange to have the moving van go to Paletón's house instead of Bellas Artes."

"Magnificent!" chanted the gangsters in unison. "Magnificent! Where there's a will, there's a way."

The moving van that arrived that night at Chapultepec Park to pick up Paco, the musical elephant, was driven by the Chicago gangsters disguised as employees of Bellas Artes Concert Hall.

The guards didn't suspect anything and even helped place the ramp so that the musical elephant could get into the moving van. Paco, the musical elephant, who had just been bathed and perfumed and was ready to go before the public and play the piano, didn't suspect anything either. He got into the truck very calmly, and when he got out, he stepped carefully, trying not to trip, thinking he was entering the concert hall. He expected at any moment to hear the applause of hundreds of spectators.

Imagine his surprise when he heard the applause of only one person! It was Paletón. Paco, the musical elephant, looked around startled. He wasn't in Bellas Artes Concert Hall. He was in the room where Paletón kept his prized collection of two hundred fifty pianos.

When he saw so many pianos, Paco couldn't hold

himself back a moment longer. He positioned his trunk and started to play, first one piano and then another, and then another. And he played and played so much that the neighbors, who couldn't sleep with all the music, called the police.

When the police entered Paletón's house, they found the musical elephant playing the piano and the owner of the house handing over five million pesos, in singles, to the Chicago gangsters.

"Three million, four hundred and twenty-five thousand, four hundred and twenty-three; three million, four hundred and twenty-five thousand, four hundred and twenty-four . . . "

Paletón and the Chicago gangsters are now in jail. Paco, the musical elephant, is still in his cage, where every once in a while he performs and gives concerts.

Mexico is the only Latin American country that borders the United States. As a result, many Mexicans are well-informed about events and trends in the United States.

Translated by Cynthia L. Ventura

A CLOWN'S STORY

by
Mario Bencastro

I t's difficult to be a clown these days. Especially since this country is in the middle of a civil war. People live thinking about death, and they have forgotten how to laugh.

Yesterday only a few people came to the circus. But it was a momentous day. When I performed my first act, there was a political demonstration in the town park. Some people stood in the doorway, unable to decide if they should come in to see the circus or if they should attend the demonstration. I sang:

"An old man ran
after a woman in a chase

She tripped on a stump
fell down on her rump
He had a big grin on his face."

But in the plaza the people were shouting:

"The people united
will never be defeated!
The people united
will never be defeated!"

The shouting went on and on. And I admit that I must have made a strange impression, because I kept pirouetting while the crowd was shouting all kinds of political slogans.

People demanded their money back at the gate, saying my act was ridiculous and that you couldn't hear anything. The tent was left completely empty. Even the circus workers decided to leave without bothering to ask for their paychecks, knowing they would be wasting their time. They knew there wasn't a cent in the money box.

Soon the police arrived to break up the demonstration. Shots could be heard. Everyone ran for cover amid cries of despair and pain, sounds of bombs exploding. I decided to close the circus. Some people found saftey inside the tents, but then the police found them and carried them away. I remained quiet in a corner, with my painted face, my multicolored balloonlike pants, and my long yellow shoes, watching the police pull and hit people who were resisting them.

"Clown, stop smiling," said the policeman. "This is no joke."

I wanted to tell him that I wasn't laughing, that a clown's painted face makes him look happy even when he is sad, but the policeman came up to me with a threatening order:

"I don't want to hear a word from you! This is no joke."

So I covered my face with my white-gloved hands. Only when I saw them leave did I dare take my hands away from my face . . . finger by finger.

Well, all of this happened yesterday. The circus was closed for the better part of the day. It didn't open at all during the evening.

Nighttime in San Salvador isn't a good time for circuses. But it is for other things: arrests, assassinations, kidnappings, bombings, and torture. Violent acts that have nothing to do with circus art.

But ladies and gentlemen, I forgot to introduce myself: My name is Cachirulo; they call me the playful clown. Actually I'm not all that special. I'm like any other run-of-the-mill circus clown. What I mean is that I do tricks with my hands, little magical acts, pirouettes, and juggling. I can jump through a fiery hoop. I can put my head in a lion's throat without being beheaded. I walk and run on a tightrope, a fairly routine act except that I do it without safety nets over the cement floor.

I'm a trapeze artist and I also do somersaults in midair. I can keep my balance while standing on only one foot on a running horse. I can do all the standard circus acts, but in addition I am a clown, which, I might also add, is the most difficult circus job.

I should emphasize something, ladies and gentlemen: I learned everything I know from my father, who was a celebrity in his time. He owned a circus with many trained animals: elephants, tigers, lions, monkeys, and horses. Of course, he had many employees. He also had a complete band with excellent musicians as well as very talented magicians and tightrope walkers. Indian snake charmers, too. He even had a fakir who locked himself up in a snake cage, a performer whose act was to survive without food for a very long time. For several months he stayed in his cage fasting and only took a sip of water each day. The audience admired and respected him for it. But he overdid it. Eventually the audience and even the circus employees started to believe that he could go without food forever, until they actually forgot about him. Seven months later they found him dead in his cage.

My father's life was the circus. He was a very famous clown. He was honored by the President of the Republic. He traveled to all important cities of Central America. Everyone looked forward to his visits: children, teenagers, and old people. These were very happy years for my father—and, I might add, the country was also going through better times. My father called these the circus's golden days.

One day, something very strange happened, though, an incident that would change my father's life and mine forever. It happened while my father was performing one of his most celebrated magic acts. Suddenly, he froze in front of the enormous crowd, and they started to boo. Luckily, a few clowns were ready to replace him and continue the act, while I took him by the arm and led him away from the arena. I must have been around twelve years old and he about fifty. I still vividly remember that moment. He looked at me with glassy eyes and smiled in a strange way. It was as though he were lost, absent. He didn't recognize anybody. He didn't say a word. We took him to the hospital and the doctor said my father had lost his mind. A few days later he was put into a mental asylum. And so, even though I was really young at the time, that is how the entire circus was passed on to me. Animals, clowns, jugglers, trapeze artists, musicians, tents, trucks, everything. I always dreamed of having a circus like my father's. But I never imagined that I would inherit it under such dramatic circumstances.

Now I visit him every Sunday. Even though he has forgotten all of his tricks and how to speak, he doesn't stop smiling. The make-believe smile of his makeup has stayed on his face. In some ways, I think, he is happy. And it seems to me that he will always be happy as long as he is sheltered from the sad reality of this country. He will always smile.

I believe that when my father was a clown it was a fairly easy job. It was a time of tranquility and people laughed a lot. I remember the sellout crowds, when thousands of people would wait in long lines, eager to see the world's greatest clown.

But for me, being a clown has been really difficult.

The economy of the country is at its very worst. It is a dark and sad time, a time of struggle when in order to survive I have had to fire my circus friends, one by one. Many chose to leave on their own when they realized people can't spend their money and time applauding clowns. I've learned that one of the acrobats became a member of the opposition, and that another clown became a member of the government's security force. How ridiculous for them to fight each other, spilling blood instead of throwing cream pies. Life is strange.

Little by little, I've had to give my animals away. The elephants were the hardest to say good-bye to. Because there was so little food, they started to look like the giraffes. I gave one to the zoo and the other died of starvation. The lions had a hard time, too. I managed to sell a few trained tigers to the zoo and they quickly became everybody's favorite animals.

So, slowly, I got rid of every animal that needed a lot of caretaking. I had to give away the monkeys because they ate too much fruit. I gave a chimpanzee away to a man from Ahuachapán who said he had a farm that would be perfect for the animal. I don't know how, but after a few days, the chimp returned to the circus. He was particularly valuable because he belonged to a nearly extinct species. But the zoo finally came to get him, too. The only animal left is my talking parrot. She's older than the hills, and she chatters as if she were still talking to my father. Her diet is simple and cheap. She eats only a little cornmeal each day. I have continued getting rid of cages, benches, tents, cars, and whatever else I can sell.

At this very moment I see the truck coming to take away the last items, which I sold for next to nothing. They are reminders of the great circus that was my father's pride and joy. For this occasion, in honor of him, I have put on the costume that he especially liked to wear during festival days. I have painted my face with bright colors and I have put on a large smile so that when they take away what is left of the circus I can appear to be happy, even though I am really attending my circus's funeral. But ladies and gentlemen, I consider myself to be a good clown, and I am not going to disappoint you with the tears from this big knot in my throat.

I have decided that when they finally take everything away from the circus and there is only a large empty space left in the park, like a big shadow, I am not going to cry, ladies and gentlemen; I promise you I'm not going to shed a single tear. Since I'm a good clown, I'll put on my tomato-red nose, my long yellow shoes and my oversized pants, and even my curly orange wig, so that I can go away with my parrot on my shoulder, my only possession and my only companion.

I will travel through all of San Salvador, all the streets of the destroyed city, until I find a friend. And it just might be that when he sees me, he will put on a smile too. A wide, pure, and innocent smile. Because when all is said and done, ladies and gentlemen, this is a clown's story and it should end with a smile.

El Salvador is a Central American country in which a civil war has been raging for over ten years.

Translated by Lori M. Carlson

Adapted from the original story "Cuento de Payaso" for this anthology with the author's permission

TARMA

by
María Rosa Fort

One afternoon late in April, which is autumn in Peru, Julian and his sister Martina were looking out at Lima's empty beaches. The wind idly blew the striped tents where, earlier in the summer, everyone changed into bathing suits, ran into the ocean, and dove into the cool and salty waters of the Pacific. Now the water was gray, empty, and uninviting. They could see the empty shores, the waves beating down tirelessly on the dark sand. "How many waves can the ocean have?" asked Julian. "How old can the ocean be?" Martina wondered.

Martina and Julian guessed at the years and

counted the waves, but just when they thought they had an answer, they realized they could still hear their watches ticking and see new waves crashing on the beach. The waves seemed endless and they couldn't imagine a city without an ocean.

That afternoon Uncle Marcelo came by to pick them up from their parents' house and take them far away to spend the Easter holidays in Tarma, the small town where he had grown up. "It's up there," he said, pointing to the mountains, "way up there, higher than the city cliffs and taller than the tall buildings that line the downtown avenues." Worried that it would be a long, cold drive, Julian and Martina bundled up under layers of woolen clothes and huddled comfortably in their uncle's old car. Each chose a favorite window in the backseat and waited impatiently for the hoarse sounds of the engine to pull them out of their neighborhood streets, out of the humidity that already announced the coming winter. It was late when they finally left Lima. Martina secretly asked the sun to set later than usual so they could drive safely up the mountains and enjoy the new sights along the way.

They soon left behind the familiar city streets. Now, outside their windows, the pale walls of suburban houses started to disappear and the dust that covered everything in Lima was replaced by rocky formations of all sizes. Suddenly, a somber river appeared on one side of the narrow road and farther ahead a cluster of fragile straw houses that seemed to bend under the weight of their television antennas. At the edge of the road, a boy with a stick in his hand was running after a skinny dog. Bushes and trees arched over the dry earth. Then Julian and Martina started to feel the mountains rise, growing steeper every minute. Soon the tall peaks enveloped them. Like a persistent worm, the car climbed the winding road up the Andes. Julian looked back and saw only mountains, more mountains, and valleys ending in darkness. The ocean was no longer there. It belonged to another world, and so did they.

Time went by slowly and they seemed to be alone on the barren soil of the Andes. Every once in a while a car or a truck would pass them, or an isolated walker would be seen steadily heading toward some hidden village behind the mountains. But for most of the drive, Uncle Marcelo's car seemed to be the only life on the silent mountains.

They finally reached the highest point on the road, where it felt as though they were at the edge of the sky, and here Martina started having the symptoms of the feared *soroche,* or altitude sickness. Julian quickly stuck some newspapers under her clothes, covering her chest with them, as his mother had suggested. Lying down in the backseat of the car, she breathed in deeply and waited for her body to get used to the dry, thin air of the Andes. The night wasn't friendly either. Darkness had set in, punctual as usual. But when the little town finally appeared in a ravine on the other side of the mountain, it was sprinkled with tiny bright lights. Outlined by the festive bulbs were the profiles of the people of Tarma curiously examining the many strangers visiting for Holy Week.

Tarma had been invaded. Lodgings proudly displayed their no-vacancy signs. But Uncle Marcelo, Julian, and Martina soon noticed that all the private homes were open and lit, their owners unfailingly standing at the doors. It was an old tradition. Families opened their arms and houses to receive, for only a few coins, those travelers who had nowhere to spend the night. Rooms that had been closed forever were now open, forgotten beds were remade, or if need be, creaking straw mats were thrown on the floor.

Uncle Marcelo, Julian, and Martina found a place in the old house of a kind lady. The rooms were set around a stone patio. In one of them, Julian and

Martina went to rest for the night. When they closed their eyes to sleep, Uncle Marcelo was still looking out the window at the town in which he was born.

Early the following morning, Julian and Martina stepped out to meet the sunny day. The clear light of the sierra surprised the two travelers, who were used to the gray sky of their city. They walked through the narrow, cobblestoned streets. As they arrived at the middle of the town square, they looked up beyond the tiled roofs of the Andean town at the openness of the sky, hills, and pastures. A strange silence came over them. But Tarma soon filled up with people preparing for the main procession of Holy Week. And when they were met by their uncle, Julian and Martina joined in this mysterious ritual.

At dusk Tarma's residents and visitors from far away gathered together in the town square to chat and stroll. They talked about the next day's main event, when the women and girls of Tarma would go to gather flowers of every imaginable color. With their baskets full and their swollen aprons resting over their thickly layered skirts, they would return to the city to cover the streets with blossoms.

At sunrise the next morning the city was empty and quiet. Martina woke up early and, while everybody was still asleep, went downstairs to the patio. She crossed it, headed toward the big wooden door, and struggled to push it open. From the threshold she watched the deserted street as though she were waiting for somebody. A girl with a basket on her arm walked past her on the other side of the street. Martina followed her in silence for quite a while until they reached the end of the town, where the mountain range began. She followed her new friend down a lush green slope that ended in a gurgling stream surrounded by a bed of flowers. There they stopped. The two girls smiled at each other and knelt on the damp grass. Together they filled the basket with petals until not one more flower could fit in it. Only then could they start on their way back.

Toward noon, Tarma came to life when all the peasant girls returned from the fields with their baskets full of flowers. Bending over the uneven cobblestones of the streets, the girls began to cover them with the colorful petals. Martina watched attentively. She noticed how carefully each girl's hands covered the cobblestones with designs made up of petals of every color. Uncle Marcelo had told her these were images of Holy Week. Soon the streets of Tarma were transformed. Petals in the shape of a llama, a quino tree, a snow-capped mountain, and even a Donald Duck figure filled the streets. The cobblestones were now covered with rugs that seemed to be made out of light and velvet where all the colors of the world blended together. Martina discovered an unexpected beauty. "Hands are magical," she thought.

Meanwhile, on the other side of the sea of flowers, Uncle Marcelo and Julian were looking for Martina. They asked the barber about her, they asked the fruit vendor, the kind lady of the house, and her neighbors. But it didn't occur to them to ask the girls who had gone to the fields to pick the flowers. They finally found Martina near the square looking at the peaceful, flowered streets.

Soon dusk was ready to fall upon the town. Uncle Marcelo, Julian, and Martina stayed together to watch the procession.

When the last rays of the sun flooded the central nave of the Cathedral, the leader of the procession gave a signal to the faithful gathered inside it. They bent their knees slightly to place on their shoulders the heavy wooden platform bearing the statue of Jesus. The members of the procession timed their steps to the rhythm of drumbeats and trumpets. Behind them the people of Tarma and the many visitors accompanied the sacred images on their slow journey through the town. As the people advanced, the delicate petals died one by one. Absorbed by the drama of the procession, Martina looked at the peasant girl's hands now folded in prayer.

For hours, while the green fields around Tarma darkened with the setting sun, the faithful continued to walk on the flowers of Tarma. The procession wound along the streets and then back inside the cathedral lit with the flickering of innumerable candles.

The celebrations were over. In the town that night, everyone dreamed quiet dreams while outside the wind swept away the last traces of the llama, the tree, the mountain, the duck. The house of the kind lady was now dark. Everybody was asleep. Across the room, Martina heard Julian breathing deeply. She closed her eyes, and when everything around her disappeared behind the smell of her alpaca blanket, she said good-bye to Tarma. As she fell asleep, she could already feel the slow whirl taking her down the tall mountains toward the foot of the Andes. And further, down to the ocean, where the waves still crashed on the dark sands of Lima.

Peru borders on the Pacific Ocean and rises dramatically to the Andes mountain range. Because Peru is below the equator, its cold and rainy winter arrives in June, just when summer begins in countries north of the equator.

Translated by Lori M. Carlson and Cynthia L. Ventura

FAIRY TALE

by
Barbara Mujica

From the bedroom window of the apartment on West 110th Street, you could see Caserta's Italian Market, López's Chino Cubano Restaurant, and Schultz's Dry Cleaners, where a black man named Ray remade the dresses of the ladies who took the subway uptown to call on him because he was the best tailor on the upper west side of Manhattan. In the summer, Ray plugged in an extension cord and dragged the sewing machine out into the street. It was only the beginning of June, but the air was hot and sultry and Ray had set up outside early that morning. He was a strange sight, sitting there on the sidewalk in front of Schultz's, clothes folded neatly in baskets on either side of him. Occasionally he looked up to wave to a neighborhood child.

Monica could see Ray stitching, stitching, stitching as she lugged the vacuum cleaner over her mother's gray carpet. It was a big household: Monica, her father, mother, and grandmother, three brothers and two sisters. Everyone had to pitch in. It was Monica's job to vacuum. She liked doing her parents' bedroom best because she could see the street as she worked. She liked watching Ray engrossed in his hemming and tacking and tucking. Except for rainy days, he always worked in the street. Monica didn't know Ray very well, but there was something comforting about his presence out there in the street.

Monica had homework to do. There was an English composition to write and a page of math. She was anxious to finish it before her mother, Angela, got home. Angela would make a fuss if she caught Monica studying. She didn't like to see her daughter with her nose in her schoolbooks. The girl was getting ideas about going to college when she should be thinking about going to a vocational school and getting a job. A beauty school would be good, Angela thought. Once she got her operator's license, Monica could get work in a beauty shop and start earning money.

Julio, her father, didn't agree. The child was smart, he told his wife. The nuns said she had a head for figures. The City University system not only was inexpensive, but gave needy students grants to pursue their studies. Monica would be foolish not to take advantage of the opportunity. She could take the subway downtown to Baruch College and get a degree in business.

But Angela thought it was a waste of time. Why should the girl be sitting in a classroom when she could be out earning money? It didn't make sense to her.

They argued about it a lot. Julio called Angela backward and small-minded. His face swelled and turned purple like an eggplant. Just when he was about to go into his stomping-out-the-door routine, Angela would rivet herself in front of him to block his way. She called him all kinds of names that were meant to hurt but which he took as compliments: dreamer, crackpot, Jesus Christ in a rattletrap jalopy.

Once she called him Don Quixote in pink suspenders. Julio had been ready to shout, but instead, he burst out laughing. He was impressed that she had heard of Don Quixote. He hadn't thought she was that sophisticated.

"Go ahead and laugh!" screamed Angela, trying

not to laugh herself. "You're sowing dreams in this girl's head that will sprout cockroaches!"

"Right, Mom. Let her go to college and before you know it, she'll be putting on airs! Thinking she's the last aspirin in the medicine cabinet!" shouted Monica's brother Floriano.

"Or the last Coca-Cola at the picnic!" thundered Tomás, her second brother.

"Or the last piece of toilet paper on the roll!" Floriano doubled over laughing.

Soon they were all roaring except Monica, who was on the brink of tears. She was only fifteen, so she didn't need to make a decision yet, but the way her parents carried on, a person would have thought that the next month's rent depended on it. No one asked Monica what she wanted, and maybe it was just as well. She knew that she would go to college, but her dreams—to be a lawyer, perhaps, or even a politician—were beyond even her father's aspirations for her.

Those bouts between her parents filled Monica with a black sadness that made her want to shrivel into a speck of dirt to be sucked up by the vacuum.

Monica dragged the heavy machine across the carpet. Her parents' bedroom was the room she liked to vacuum best. Sunlight flooded the freshly painted walls, the twenty-five-year-old wedding pictures, the crucifix, and the plastic flowers in the green plastic pencil holder that served as a vase. The rest of the apartment was dark, with gloomy hallways and shadowy corners. The living room was dismal despite Angela's efforts to brighten it up with pictures of matadors and dancers and roses. On one wall there was a poster of San Juan that showed a luminous patio through a wrought-iron gate. On one side of the patio there was a lemon tree with delicate white blossoms. Angela said you could almost smell the fragrance of lemons, but Monica couldn't smell anything and found her mother's nostalgia irritating.

In the kitchen, her sister Jasmín was frying onions. Monica stopped vacuuming and cupped her hand over her nose to block out the smell. *"Qué horrible,"* she muttered. Tomás and Floriano were playing marbles on the kitchen floor. The roll of the glass balls against the concrete floor sounded like thunder with the vacuum cleaner off. The boys were bickering.

"The green one is mine!"

"No, it's mine! I won it from you!"

"¡Ladrón! ¡Mentiroso!"

"You're the one who's lying."

Monica turned on the machine again to drown them out. She finished vacuuming the hallway, then put the vacuum cleaner into the closet.

She went into the room she shared with Jasmín and gathered up her books.

"I'm going downstairs," she said to Jasmín.

"With your books?"

"I need a change of scenery."

"Maybe you should set up shop on the sidewalk, like Ray."

"Maybe. Better out there in the sunlight than in this dingy apartment."

The children's grandmother was crocheting at the kitchen table.

"You want a change of scenery? Come, I'll tell you a story."

"I have no time for fairy tales, Grandma. I have a composition to write."

The old woman shrugged. Monica realized she had made her feel bad.

"Maybe tonight, Grandma. After I get done with my homework."

Her grandmother's stories were a source of both pleasure and fear to Monica. They were somber tales, filled with wraiths and shadows. In the evening, when she had finished her chores and her studies, Monica would join her brothers and sisters in the living room, where they would gather around 'Buelita Adriana and listen to tales she had heard in Puerto Rico half a century before. It was a habit. Even now that Monica was a young woman, she enjoyed her grandmother's accounts of the terrible Tía Odelia, who, after all the members of the household were asleep, would break into a thousand pieces and fly out the window into the night sky, only to return again by dawn, whole, but always with an eye or a finger or even her entire head out of place; or about the Temptress of the Waters, a beautiful enchantress who offered candy to the little children who went wandering through the woods, then nabbed them and dragged them down to the bottom of the river, where they lived forever among the snails and aquatic plants.

Sometimes 'Buelita Adriana wove stories about La Llorona, an exquisite weeping woman who turned up in all kinds of strange places. Some people met her at night on dark, lonely roads. Some stumbled upon her in old, deserted houses. The moment anyone touched her, she would turn into a terrifying white skeleton with long, clawlike fingernails, paralyzing her victims with fear.

'Buelita Adriana had a voice like rich molasses that

soothed and ensnared Monica. The soft descriptions of the crying woman's luminous skin, her dazzling hair, the tears glistening on her cheeks, lulled the girl into a kind of trance that La Llorona's transformation exploded brutally.

No matter how many times she heard them, the stories always left Monica shaken and somber. Adriana knew just how to alter the details in order to throw her listener off guard. She had spent a lifetime getting her stories just right.

"Don't be frightened," she would say after the telling was over. "They're just folk legends. They're like fairy tales. You don't believe in fairy tales, do you?"

Monica would sit hunched and trembling in the dark room until at last the spell wore off. Then she would pull herself up and make her way into the kitchen, where she would flip the switches until every corner was lit and the shadows were gone.

The school year was almost over and the youngsters were making plans for the summer. Jasmín wanted to get a job. Monica's older brother Andrés worked in construction and thought he could get Jasmín a secretarial position with the company, whose regular secretary was going on vacation for part of the summer. Tomás and Floriano were too young to do much of anything. They would shoot marbles in the street and basketballs in the school yard for three months. Monica wasn't old enough to get a full-time job legally, but her mother thought the girl could hang around the beauty shop on Broadway and 111th. Angela had a friend there named Providencia, who had promised to teach Monica to be a shampoo girl.

"Let her go to summer school," said Julio.

"There he goes again! The emperor of China with his fly wide open! What's the matter with this man? Doesn't he see he's ridiculous?" Angela was talking to the dishes as she set the table.

"What's so ridiculous?"

"We don't have the money, Julio. You think you're Napoleon, but you're only a janitor!"

"How do you know about Napoleon?"

"I saw a movie on TV. You think you're the only one who knows something around here? You don't know from *habichuelas*, Julio. You've always got your head in the clouds."

"It would be good if the kid went to summer school. She could learn something. She could get ahead."

"Catholic schools cost money. Let her go to a public school. At least for the summer."

"I don't want my kid in no public school. They're

smoking crack in the hallways in the public schools."

"Look," interrupted Monica. "I have an idea. I've been thinking about it for a long time. What if I went to Puerto Rico for the summer? I've never been there. You and 'Buelita are always talking about it."

The first part wasn't true. Monica had not been thinking about it for a long time. It had occurred to her that morning when she looked out the window and saw Ray sitting and sewing in the sun. Monica had never been particularly interested in Puerto Rico. She associated the birthplace of her parents and grandmother with fried onions and black beans, both of which made her feel bloated and gassy. Puerto Rico was what her relatives had wanted to get away from: bad landlords, poverty, superstition, unemployment, bare feet, and outside toilets. In New York, her parents had not found wealth, but they both had jobs and the family managed. Julio was a doorman during the day and a janitor at night. Sometimes he drove a delivery truck on the weekends. Angela was on the cleaning crew at Grand Central Station. They paid their bills and kept their children out of trouble.

Monica's life in New York was tolerable most of the time and agreeable some of the time, but the apartment was depressing. Monica imagined herself outdoors, like Ray, working at a table piled high with books. She imagined herself an attorney, a well-known public defender, worshipped by a community that begged her to run for councilwoman, sitting at a card table in the middle of the sidewalk, with her research materials spread everywhere. She laughed to herself at the thought of her father coming home to the apartment after a day guarding the door at the huge, expensive white building on Seventh Avenue, only to find his daughter, dressed in a business suit and sensible shoes, set up in the middle of 110th Street, surrounded by contracts and wills.

"I'm sorry," she would say, "but I can't move, Daddy. I need the light."

She did need the light. She imagined her parents' village in Puerto Rico bathed in a light so bright it hurt your eyes. She imagined sugarcane, palm trees, bananas, and tropical flowers of reds, pinks, oranges, and yellows, all bright beneath the sun.

Angela was the first to react to Monica's unexpected suggestion.

"It would be expensive," she said.

"Maybe we could work something out," said 'Buelita Adriana. "I have about four hundred dollars I could let her have. It would be good for the child.

Besides, Pedro and Carmen are always saying they'd love to have her."

"She couldn't study," piped up Julio.

"No, but she'd be learning. She'd be learning about her past, about where she came from. Maybe she'd learn some more Spanish."

"We could put her on a plane at Kennedy," said Angela. "Pedro and Carmen could meet her at the airport in San Juan."

Julio was silent a moment. "Well," he said finally, "I suppose it would be all right. I would like her to meet her relatives in Puerto Rico. I just hope she won't come back *hecha una jíbara.*"

"*El jíbaro ereh tú,*" snapped Angela. "You're the hick."

Monica was dizzy with excitement. She had never traveled anywhere before, except to Atlantic City and on the subway to Coney Island.

The whole family went to the airport to see Monica off, even Andrés, who took a day off his construction job. 'Buelita Adriana had packed sandwiches and fruit for the plane ride, even though she knew the stewardesses would serve lunch. She and Angela had filled a suitcase with everything from plastic combs to Bon Jovi records to a small artificial Christmas tree, left over from last December, for the relatives in Puerto Rico. Angela, whose mouth normally worked like a submachine gun, was quiet and teary. Everyone kissed Monica over and over. Only the younger boys were playful.

"Hey, Sis," teased Tomás, "don't let La Llorona get you."

Monica laughed.

"Please, don't talk to me about that rubbish! I'm nervous enough . . . the first time on a plane."

"It won't crash, Sis. Grandma cast a spell on it."

By the time she boarded the plane, Monica was glad to get away from her noisy family.

Aunt Carmen, Uncle Pedro, and their daughter Modesta met Monica at the San Juan airport. Then they all got on a bus that would take them to the same small village in which Monica's parents and grandmother had been born.

During the entire first month, Monica was radiant. Her aunt and uncle were hardworking, but easygoing. They joked constantly, teasing each other and Modesta. They still worked the cane fields, but they had built a nice little stucco house with the money that Julio had sent them over the years. The outside walls were white; the inside walls were assorted pastels. There was a fair-sized garden with palm trees and a lemon tree that Monica could actually smell, and all kinds of brilliantly hued flowers. The brightness of the garden filled Monica with excitement. She could stand in the middle of the blossoms, close her eyes, and feel the colors, warm on her skin.

Monica had chores, just like her cousin, but they were different from the ones she had in New York. She fed the chickens and helped with the other animals. She swept the patio and weeded the garden. She was always outside. Sometimes she played with the younger children, daughters and sons of her Aunt Estela, who also lived in the village. Sometimes she got a book and sat under a tree and read it. Her relatives laughed at her broken Spanish and admired her ability to read English. On the weekends there were parties, with beer and music and dancing. Monica was so busy she almost forgot about New York, her family's dingy apartment, her brothers' bickering, and her grandmother's stories.

Monica had noticed from the beginning that there was something wrong with Modesta's foot. It turned inward and caused the girl great pain when she put her weight on it. Once a month Aunt Carmen and Uncle Pedro made the trek to San Juan to have a doctor at a public clinic treat it.

"We'll be leaving early in the morning," Aunt Carmen told Monica the day before their monthly excursion, "and we'll be gone all day. We can't take you with us, but you can stay with Estela if you like."

Monica hesitated only a moment.

"Can't I stay here, Aunt Carmen? I'm not afraid to be alone."

"I know you're not, *hijita.* Of course you can stay here. We'll try to be back before dark. There's plenty in the cupboards for you to eat. Don't forget to feed those silly goats. Otherwise, they'll eat the screens off the windows."

"Don't worry, Aunt Carmen."

The day passed quickly. Monica loved being alone in the house. She sat on the patio, her books spread around her, and read for hours. She attended to the animals and to the garden. She climbed up onto the fence in order to reach a bunch of bananas and a papaya growing near the house.

But as night grew near, Monica began to feel jittery. Shadows were forming on the walls, and Monica remembered 'Buelita Adriana's scary folk legends, especially the one about La Llorona.

"Rubbish," she said to herself. "Those stories are to frighten little children into behaving. They're more superstitious at home than here, on the island." For a moment, she felt herself back in New York, in the dim living room of her apartment, huddled up, shuddering from one of her grandmother's tales.

"Rubbish," she whispered again. "Stories to give little children nightmares."

The sun was going down. Monica went out to check on the chickens and the other animals.

"There's nothing to worry about," she thought. "After all, they said they might be late."

Outside, shadows grew and multiplied and melted into one another. Monica thought it was too late to walk over to Aunt Estela's. In a few minutes she wouldn't even be able to see the road.

Monica checked the door—there was only one— although she knew that Aunt Carmen and Uncle Pedro rarely locked it.

"This is silly," she said to herself. "Why am I so fidgety?" She made a sandwich and carried it into the living room. Monica put her half-eaten sandwich down beside her on a little wooden table and closed her eyes and dozed.

A few minutes later she awakened with a start.

"What was that?" she said to herself. "I thought I heard something."

She stood up and walked to the window. She

peered out, but saw only the silhouettes of trees and bushes against the dark sky.

There was a rustling. It sounded like a small animal—a cat, maybe—brushing against vegetation. And then, a soft whimpering.

Monica groped for the only lamp in the room and felt for the switch. The bulb cast a soft, eerie glow over the sofa.

"I shouldn't have turned on the light," she said to herself. "If there's a person out there, he'll see me."

Then she heard it again: a moan or a cry.

"It must be a lost child," she thought. She opened the door gently and cast her gaze over the dark patio. Something moved. She could hear it clearly now. Someone was sobbing in the darkness.

In the near blackness, Monica could just make out the figure of a girl seated on the ground. She appeared to be a little older than Monica herself, although it was difficult to see her features. Her head was bowed, her face covered with her hands. She had thrown a dark shawl over her shoulders, but her light hair was exposed. A basket of flowers lay by her side.

Monica forgot caution and approached the girl.

"What's the matter?" she asked. "Can I help you? Are you lost?"

The girl didn't answer. She simply continued crying as though her heart would break.

"Please," said Monica. "Let me help you."

Slowly the girl lifted her face and looked at Monica. She appeared to be older than Monica had originally thought. Perhaps she was twenty or twenty-two. Her lips were full and moist. In the dim light, her eyes shone huge. They were filled with tears.

The young woman swallowed as if she were trying to speak.

"I don't know what to do," she said finally. "I seem to have lost my way. I must have taken a wrong turn somewhere back on the road. And now it's dark." She was clutching a bunch of tiny purple flowers. Monica thought that they seemed somehow out of place. Their subdued violet hue was different from the cheerful shades that filled her aunt's garden.

"Do you want to call someone? We have a phone."

"It's too late for anyone to come and get me. Anyhow, they won't want to see me. I haven't earned a cent today. They'll be angry. I was trying to sell these flowers. They're not expensive, but people don't spend money on flowers. Why should they? The gardens are full of flowers. Although these in particular are very rare. Anyway, I haven't sold a single bunch. And now I have no money and no place to go."

"Poor thing," said Monica. "Aunt Carmen and Uncle Pedro will be home soon. I'm sure they'll buy something from you. In the meantime, come in and let me get you something to eat."

The young woman lowered her eyes as though she were embarrassed to accept Monica's invitation.

"Thank you," she said almost inaudibly. "You're very kind. I have nothing to give you in return but this bouquet of flowers. Please take it. It's all I can offer you to show my appreciation."

"There's no need . . . "

"Please," said the young woman.

"Thank you." Monica reached out her hand.

The movement and the blood-chilling scream were simultaneous. Monica's arm snapped back as though it were a whip that, cracked by a horseman, returns automatically. She cringed and tried to draw away, but her legs had turned icy and stiff. Shivering with fear, tears gushing down her cheeks and neck, Monica stood transfixed by the image before her. In the place of the young woman stood a ghoulish skeleton, glimmering and horrible. Long, bony fingers with clawlike fingernails beckoned hideously.

Monica let out another protracted scream. Her legs regained their strength. She ran away from the house, past the garden, past the village, into the cane fields. It seemed to her that she ran for an eternity. Her chest felt pinched, but still she ran. Her lungs felt as though they were filled with broken glass. Her breathing became more and more jagged. Her legs ached and her knees smarted, but still she ran. Behind her hovered the terrible specter. She sensed its presence in the smothering darkness.

At last, she stumbled and fell heavily onto the ground. Who knows how long she lay there. It must have been a long, long time.

Suddenly, Monica opened her eyes and looked around. She was in the bedroom she shared with Modesta in her aunt and uncle's house. The curtains were open and the walls were bathed in light. In the kitchen, Aunt Carmen was singing *"Solamente una Vez"* as she prepared breakfast.

"My God," shuddered Monica. "I had an awful nightmare."

The leaves and flowers were brilliant in the sunshine. The fragrance of lemon filled the fresh, clean air.

Monica smiled. "It was only a dream," she said out loud.

"It must have been a terrible one!" responded Modesta. For some reason she was carrying a tray with breakfast on it, which she placed on the night table next to Monica.

Monica looked at her in astonishment.

"What's this?"

"Mom wants you to eat. You've been sleeping for hours and hours. What happened to you?"

"I had . . . I had a nightmare."

"A nightmare! We found you in the middle of a cane field sound asleep! The whole village was out looking for you. We brought you back here and put you to bed."

Monica opened her eyes wide. The gnawing in her stomach had begun again. She stared at her cousin in disbelief.

"You were clutching those."

On the night table lay a bouquet of tiny purple flowers.

During the 1940s and 1950s there was a large Puerto Rican migration to New York. Many Puerto Ricans who have settled on the mainland still travel frequently to their native island.

A HUGE BLACK UMBRELLA

by
Marjorie Agosín

When she arrived at our house she was covered by a huge black umbrella. A white gardenia hung from her left ear. My sister Cynthia and I were bewitched by the sight of her. We were a little afraid, too. She seemed like an enormous fish or a shipwrecked lady far from home. Certainly, her umbrella was useless in the rain since it was ripped in many places, which let the rainwater fall on her—water from one of the few downpours of that surprisingly dry summer. It was the summer in which my sister and I understood why magical things happen, such as the arrival of Delfina Nahuenhual.

My mother welcomed her, and Delfina, with a certain boldness, explained that she always traveled accompanied by that enormous umbrella, which protected her from the sun, elves, and little girls like us. My mother's delicate lips smiled. From that moment my mother and Delfina developed a much friendlier relationship than is usual between "the lady of the house" and "her servant."

Delfina Nahuenhual—we had to call her by her full name—was one of the few survivors of the Chillán earthquake in the south of Chile. She had lost her children, house, her wedding gown, chickens, and two of her favorite lemon trees. All she could rescue was that huge black umbrella covered with dust and forgotten things.

In the evening she usually lit a small stove for cooking; the fire gave off a very lovely, sweet light. Then she wrapped herself up in an enormous shawl of blue wool that wasn't scratchy and she put a few slices of potato on her temples to protect herself from sickness and cold drafts.

As we sat by the stove, Delfina Nahuenhual told stories about tormented souls and frogs that became princes. Her generous lap rocked us back and forth, and her voice made us sleepy. We were peaceful children who felt the healing power of her love. After she thought we were asleep, Delfina Nahuenhual would write long letters that she would later number and wrap up in newspaper. She kept the letters in an old pot that was filled with garlic, cumin, and slivers of lemon rind.

My sister and I always wanted to read those letters and learn the name and address of the person who would receive them. So whenever Delfina Nahuenhual was busy in the kitchen, we tried peeking into the pot to discover what she was hiding.

But we never managed to read the letters. Delfina Nahuenhual would smile at us and shoo us along with the end of her broom.

For many years, Delfina continued to tell us stories next to the stove. Not long after my brother Mario, the spoiled one of the family, was born, Delfina Nahuenhual told us that she was tired and that she wanted to return to the south of Chile. She said she now had some savings and a chicken, which was enough to live on. I thought that she wanted to die and go to heaven because she had decided to return to the mosses and clays of her land.

I remember that I cried a lot when we said good-bye. My brother Mario clung to her full skirt, not wanting to be separated from the wise woman who, for us, was never a servant. When she bent over to give me a kiss, she said that I must give her letters to the person to whom she had addressed them but that I could keep the pot.

For many years, I kept her little pot like a precious secret, a kind of magical lamp in which my childhood was captured. When I wanted to remember her, I rubbed the pot, I smelled it, and all my fears, including my fear of darkness, vanished. After she left I began to understand that my childhood had gone with her. Now more than ever I miss the dish of lentils that she prepared for good luck and prosperity on New Year's Eve. I miss the smell of her skin and her magical stories.

Many years later, my sister Cynthia had her first daughter. Mario went traveling abroad and I decided to spend my honeymoon on Easter Island, that remote island in the middle of the Pacific Ocean, six hours by plane from Chile. It is a place full of mysterious, gigantic statues called Moais. Ever since I was a child, I had been fascinated by those eerie statues, their enormous figures seeming to spring from the earth, just as Delfina Nahuenhual and her huge black umbrella did when she first came to my house. I carried her letters, which I had long ago taken from the small earthen pot and placed in a large moss-green chest along with the few cloves of garlic that still remained. As a grown-up I never had the urge to read the letters. I only knew that they should be delivered to someone.

One morning when the sun shone even in the darkest corner of my hotel room, I went to the address written on Delfina's letters. It was a leper colony, one of the few that still exist. A very somber employee opened the door and quickly took the packet of five hundred letters from me. I asked if the addressee was still alive and he said of course, but that I couldn't meet the person. When I gave him the letters, it seemed as though I had lost one of my most valuable possessions, perhaps even the last memories of my dear Delfina Nahuenhual's life.

So I never did meet the person to whom Delfina Nahuenhual wrote her letters nor learned why she spent her sleepless nights writing them. I only learned that he was a leper on Easter Island, that he was still alive and, perhaps, still reads the letters, the dreams of love Delfina Nahuenhual had each night. When I returned home, I knew at last that Delfina Nahuenhual was content, because when I looked up, as she had taught me to do, I saw a huge black umbrella hovering in the cloudy sky.

Chile has suffered many disasters, some natural and some political, and Chileans have had to do their best to rebuild their lives wherever they have relocated.

Translated by Lori M. Carlson

GLOSSARY

"The Day We Went to See Snow"
SAN JUAN—The capital city of Puerto Rico
BAYAMÓN—City in Puerto Rico west of San Juan
SANTURCE—One of the oldest sectors in San Juan
BRIDGES IN CONDADO—During the early years of the Spanish conquest, the capital city of San Juan was a small island very near the main island of Puerto Rico. These bridges were built to connect San Juan to Puerto Rico and are important landmarks in the city.
GUAYABERA—A loose man's shirt with a pleated front worn in Latin America, especially those countries with warm climates

"With My Eyes Closed"
ORIENTE—Eastern province in Cuba

"Paletón and the Musical Elephant"
CHAPULTEPEC PARK—A large park and zoo in Mexico City
PESO—Mexican money
BELLAS ARTES—A performing arts center in Mexico City

"A Clown's Story"
AHUACHAPÁN—Province and town northwest of San Salvador, the capital city of El Salvador

"Tarma"
TARMA—Town located in the Peruvian Andes
LIMA—Capital city of Peru, located on the Pacific coast
QUINO—A tree found in Peru whose bark is used to produce quinine

"Fairy Tale"
DON QUIXOTE—The idealistic and misguided hero in the classic Spanish novel of the same name published by Miguel de Cervantes Saavedra in 1605 and 1615
LADRÓN—Thief
MENTIROSO—Liar

'BUELITA—Abbreviated form of *abuelita*, grand-mother
TÍA—Aunt
LA LLORONA—The weeper
HABICHUELAS—Beans
HECHA UNA JÍBARA—Acting like a hillbilly
HIJITA—Little daughter (used as a term of endear-ment)
"SOLAMENTE UNA VEZ"—"Only Once," title of an old ballad

"A Huge Black Umbrella"
CHILLÁN—Town in southern Chile
EASTER ISLAND—Island located in the South Pacific Ocean west of Chile known for its unusual hiero-glyphs and gigantic carved heads. Though thou-sands of miles from Latin America, the island is controlled by Chile.

ABOUT THE AUTHORS

Marjorie Agosín, a Chilean poet and essayist, is a professor of Spanish at Wellesley College in Massachusetts. She has written many books of poetry, among them *Zones of Pain*, and numerous books about the lives of Latin American women.

Isabel Allende is one of Latin America's best-known novelists. Originally from Chile, she currently lives in the United States. Her first novel, *The House of the Spirits*, is perhaps still her most-admired work.

Reinaldo Arenas was born in Holguín, Cuba, and has lived in the United States since 1980. He has published many novels and collections of short stories, including *Farewell to the Sea* and *Graveyard of Angels*.

Mario Bencastro is a writer and painter who was born in Ahuachapán, El Salvador, and now lives in the United States. He has written poetry, plays, and a prize-winning novel, *Disparo en la Catedral* (A Shot in the Cathedral).

Julio Cortázar, an Argentine born in Brussels, lived for many years in Paris working as a translator, fiction writer, and poet. Many of his books have been published in English; these include *Hopscotch* and *Cronopios and Famas*. Julio Cortázar died in Paris in 1984.

Ariel Dorfman is a Chilean author and human rights activist. He is currently Research Professor of Literature and Latin American Studies at Duke University. Many of his works have been published in English; they include *The Empire's Old Clothes* and his most recent novel, *Mascara*.

María Rosa Fort has done graduate work in Latin American literature at Columbia University. She is a Peruvian psychologist who has worked as a psychotherapist in Peru and France. She has also published translations of Latin American writers.

Jorge Ibargüengoitia, a Mexican writer, wrote *The Dead Girls* and several other novels as well as many children's stories. In 1983 he, along with several other Latin American writers, died in a tragic plane crash.

Enrique Jaramillo Levi was born in Colón, Panama, and now is a professor of Latin American literature. His publications include collections of poetry and short stories, the most well-known being *Duplicaciones* (Duplications) (1989).

Barbara Mujica, a North American writer, is a professor of Spanish at Georgetown University in Washington, D.C., and is the author of many articles about Latin America and a novel, *The Deaths of Don Bernardo.* Her stories have appeared in anthologies and magazines throughout the United States.

Alfredo Villanueva-Collado is a poet and short story writer who was born in San Juan, Puerto Rico. He has written several collections of poetry in Spanish, including *El Imperio de la Papa Frita* (The Empire of the French Fry) (1988).

ABOUT THE EDITORS

Lori M. Carlson received an M.A. in Latin American literature from Indiana University, Bloomington. She is a former managing editor of *Review: Latin American Literature and Arts* magazine, and she is now a consulting editor for a Spanish-language book club.

Cynthia L. Ventura received an M.A. in Comparative Literature and Translation Studies at the State University of New York at Binghamton. She is a translator/interpreter in the New York City court system and has translated works by many Latin American writers.

ACKNOWLEDGMENTS

We gratefully acknowledge the following:

Agencia Literaria Carmen Balcells, S.A., for "Paletón and the Musical Elephant" by Jorge Ibargüengoitia. Copyright © Heirs of Jorge Ibargüengoitia, 1989.

Marjorie Agosín for her story "A Huge Black Umbrella." Copyright © 1990 by Marjorie Agosín. Reprinted by her permission.

Reinaldo Arenas for his story "With My Eyes Closed." Copyright © 1990 by Reinaldo Arenas. Reprinted by his permission.

Mario Bencastro for his story "A Clown's Story." Copyright © 1990 by Mario Bencastro. Reprinted by his permission.

Ariel Dorfman for his story "The Rebellion of the Magical Rabbits." Copyright © 1990 by Ariel Dorfman. Reprinted by his permission.

María Rosa Fort for her story "Tarma." Copyright © 1990 by María Rosa Fort. Reprinted by her permission.

Enrique Jaramillo Levi for his story "The Cave." Copyright © 1990 by Enrique Jaramillo Levi. Reprinted by his permission.

Barbara Mujica for her story "Fairy Tale." Copyright © 1990 by Barbara Mujica. Reprinted by her permission.